Sexual Healing

Jacquie Murrell

Published by Leo's Print, Inc
P.O. Box 881252
Indianapolis, IN 46208
www.leosprintinc.com
ISBN-13: 978-0-692-06520-4

DEDICATION

Have you ever looked someone in the eye or saw a picture of them years later and were asked by someone else if you knew them and replied no, only to remember days later that you do because you slept with them? Well, what if I told you that I have, and honestly could not remember who they were?

I wanted to be desired, to be needed, to feel secure, to be validated, to be touched, to be held, to be loved, and to be healed. Sex was my 2nd choice of drug to satisfy a seemingly unquenchable thirst. You might be thinking…..this woman has daddy issues or she might be a whore. That may have been true at one point in time, but I guarantee there is something that probably did not cross your mind; sexual deviancy. This is a story of how I used sex as an interchangeable feeling with love and how doing so cost me my ability to make rational decisions and caused me to participate in the further destruction of my emotional and mental state. Rock with me, it's about to get raw and uncomfortable.

This book is dedicated to all of the young ladies and women who were or are looking for love in all of the wrong places, who feel they are too damaged to ever experience true love, and who feel they have to settle for sidepiece or main chick titles to be wanted and kept by a man. The dedication also extends to the men who want to love her but have a hard time connecting with her heart. Most importantly, to Mark Brooks, who has made it his business to be my……LOVE FINALLY.

CONTENTS

1 SEXPEDITION

Albert, Damon, Quincy, Joe, Lee, Melvin, Tom, Dante, Nathan, Brian, Ty, Paul, Damarcus, and Greg were all a part of the sexpedition between the ages of 11 and 15. Now, they were a part of the experimenting phase of this quest. You know what I mean; the prelude to or foreplay of sex, but not the act itself, with the exception of Brian, Melvin and Paul. They were a part of the act itself as well. Yes, something triggered this quest but we'll get to that later.

Between these ages, I was trying to find love, acceptance, and identity. I needed something to make me feel good about myself, wanted, valued, and needed. I didn't feel this way before I turned 11 years old. Yes, I had daddy issues, but not to the extent that I would embark upon this type of journey solely because of that. This sexpedition would last for years well beyond the age of 15, but triggered by events far more serious than daddy issues.

Imagine being in school and allowing boys to touch your vagina, breasts, and butt while fully clothed. When I wore dresses or skirts, this made for easy access. Believe it or not, about 80 percent of the time, they did not ask permission first, but it was embedded in my mind that it was something I was supposed to allow and shouldn't say anything about. How? Why? We will get to that later, but the more they did it, the more I became accustomed to it. Whether it was running up and smacking or grabbing my butt or breasts and running away and thinking it was funny or daring me to let them have their way or just asking and reassuring I would keep it a secret. I even recall seeing one of my parents having sex in a car in broad daylight at a park while children were playing among other things I was exposed to.

I let them touch me because their interest made me feel wanted and their compliments made me feel pretty. Yes, I participated in this activity. I let them touch me during movie time in class when the lights were off, went into supply closets when the teacher left the room and left a student in charge, and even on the bus ride home from school.

Because I could mask this very well, nobody knew. I was one of the most popular girls in school. I was in all of the choirs, a solo singer, won talents shows years in a row, made the newspapers, on student counsel, high performing athlete, and an honor student and yet, I was hurting inside. Looking back, I was trying to find my identity and fill voids that I did not know couldn't be filled through those activities. I kissed and allowed boys to fondle me at 11 ½ years old.

Did I just wake up one day and decide this would be the kind of girl I wanted to be? Had I been a "fast tail" from a very little girl up until this point? No. What happened?

SEX HYPE:

As an adult trying to heal self from the pain of the past, I had to go back and find the root of my corrupted mindset and unstable emotional state. I realized the corruption of my mindset and innocence played a large role in how I saw myself as a woman, the type of men I chose and why I spent many years using sex to get over life's mayhem.

During my pre-teen and teenage years, I realized that even though I was told how pretty I was often and was cheered for by many for my accomplishments, it still wasn't enough. It was almost like I needed proof that these things were true and because of one encounter that started it all, my sexpedition began and became an addiction that grew too strong to satisfy.

Looking back, I now know I did not need to engage in that type of activity as it added to my already fragile state. It caused me to become more confused about who I was, what love was, and how to get out of the hell I was in. So, to every young lady struggling with embarking on their own sexpedition, do not allow yourself to be further violated by roaming hands for the sake of "feeling" wanted or loved. You must take the necessary steps towards understanding who you are and what true love is so you KNOW what that looks like. When this happens, you will be in a better position to receive it and give it, but understand that it has nothing to do with sexual acts or sex itself.

2 SEXUAL DEVIANCY

"When I was 11 years old, I stayed the night at a friend's house who happened to be my best friend at that time. While staying over this particular weekend, my friend's mother (who we will call Ms. Smith) invited some friends over. They were talking and playing cards while my friend and I along with her 2 brothers were watching television. It was late so we were all in our pajamas. I was wearing a red thick cotton, long sleeved, ankle length night gown with a pocket across the chest area. After some time had passed, Ms. Smith's friends left except for one and this particular friend brought another friend. They were both men. Ms. Smith, her daughter, the two men, myself and the oldest brother began playing Go Fish. The youngest brother fell asleep and got up to lie down in his room. Ms. Smith's friend said he had to leave for a little while and he would be back. He left the friend he invited with us. The man reeked of alcohol and we could tell that he was extremely drunk. He looked to be about 30 to 37 years old. He was a light skinned man, about 5'7" with curly dark hair and a trimmed beard. I will never forget the way he looked.

As we continued to play cards, we struck up a conversation and the man told us that he had a daughter and showed us a picture. He also said that he had just got out of jail but he never told us what he was in jail for. Ms. Smith and her son began to get sleepy so we all stopped playing cards. Ms. Smith and her daughter stretched out on the couches and watched television until they fell asleep. Ms. Smith's son and I sat on the floor and watched television. The stranger sat across the room on the floor and watched television with us.

Ms. Smith's son nudged me and told me to look over to my left. The stranger was staring at me. It made me feel uneasy and a little scared. Tim and I knew something wasn't right about him. Tim told the stranger to call his friend to come and get him because he wanted to lock up the house. The stranger said he didn't know how to contact his friend and that he would just wait until his friend returned. It was about two o'clock in the morning.

A few minutes later, the stranger began to whisper to me, saying, "Come here." I looked at the stranger and told him no and then turned back to look at the television. I was very afraid now. Tim told the man to leave me alone but he just kept on whispering to me. Tim was about 8 or 9 years old and like I said before, I was 11 years old, so the stranger really wasn't listening to us. Tim and I looked over at the couches at Ms. Towns and Alisha. The stranger knew that we were thinking about waking them. The stranger told us to be quiet in a firm tone. We were afraid. Tim and I were no longer sleepy. Now we were wide awake because we knew the stranger was drunk, had just gotten out of jail, and was up to no good.

I continued to ignore the stranger whispering to me. About five minutes later, the stranger slid across the floor over to me and grabbed me by my arm and drug me over to where he was sitting. I was instantly overcome by fear. I began to tremble. Tim told the stranger to leave me alone. The stranger told Tim to be quiet and said, "I'm not going to hurt her." The stranger was sitting on the floor with his legs straddled and he pulled me close to him so that my back was lying against his stomach. He wrapped his arms around me. I began to tremble all over and tears began to run down my face. I didn't utter a sound. I was so scared that I couldn't say anything. I was frozen with fear. I had never been so scared before. I thought if I screamed, he would hurt me or Tim. He whispered in my ear and asked me, "Why are you shaking?" He said, "I'm not going to hurt you." "Stop Shaking", he said.

Tim sat very still in front of the television. He looked like he was thinking of what to do to help me. In my mind, I wished that he would hurry up and think of something. I tried to get loose from the stranger's grip but he just pulled me closer and wrapped his arms around me tighter. I just knew he was going to hurt me. He kept his left arm around my left shoulder and left side of my neck. He began to slide his right hand down inside the top of my night gown and began to fondle me by rubbing his hand across my breasts. It felt like I was trembling so much that you would think I was having a seizure. Tim looked over and saw what the stranger was doing to me and Tim's face turned angry. He went into deep thought. I imagine he was thinking about how to save me. The stranger continued to fondle my breasts and tears continued to pour down my face and I still didn't utter a word. The stranger took his hand out of my nightgown and began to stroke my stomach. I trembled in more fear. I just knew what he was going to do next. He placed his left hand around my waist and held me still. He took his right hand and placed it on my vaginal area. I don't know what happened, but something in me couldn't let him go further. Tim looked at me and knew I was about to do something. I was still very afraid but I had to try and escape again before my innocence was ripped from my body.

I jumped up and the stranger grabbed my arm and asked, "What are you doing?" "Where are you going?" he asked. I thought of something quick and said, "I'm going to the restroom." I ran to the restroom and Tim ran to his room. I tried to lock the door but there was no lock on it. I was pacing back and forth thinking about what to do next. I was crying and trembling. I heard someone coming down the hall. I backed up against the bathroom wall. The door opened and it was the stranger. He asked me what I was doing in the bathroom. I ran out past him and into Alisha's room. Ms. Towns and Alisha was still sleep. They couldn't hear anything because Tim and I were quiet like the man told us to be because we thought he would definitely hurt us. Our need to get rid of him was stronger than our fear now.

Alisha's room was pitch black. I thought I could hide in there. She didn't have enough space under the bed for me to crawl under it. The closet had too much stuff in it for me to fit in there so I laid down flat in her bed and pulled the covers over my face. I prayed he didn't see where I went. He was drunk so he was moving kind of slow and staggering. I heard a noise in the next room. It was Tim. He was in his room looking for something.

While I lay in the pitch black room under the covers, I remembered my grandma praying and teaching me how to pray to ask

God for whatever I needed. I was still so scared. I was still crying and trembling and tried to stay quiet so the stranger wouldn't find me. I began to pray. I said, "God please don't let this man find me and get me."

I heard Alisha's door open slowly. I peeked out from the side of the covers. It was the stranger. I got back under the cover and I heard the door close. I thought he left. I looked out from under the cover and he was standing in the room. It was still dark. He began taking off his shoes and his clothes by the door. I sat so still in the bed in fear. I thought if I got up to run again, he would stop me because he was right by the door. So I waited. He undressed down to his boxers and walked around to the other side of the bed and he got in the bed and laid down next to me. He tried to put his arm around me and I jumped up and darted out of the room back into the living room. Tim was waiting with his soft ball bat. He stood guard at the end of the hallway while I tried to wake Alisha and Ms. Towns. I tried to wake them quickly and quietly so the stranger wouldn't hear us. I began to shake my friend to wake her. I was crying and frantic. I was begging her to get up. Tim told me to hurry. The stranger was coming out of the room but he was half dressed. Alisha jumped up and asked what was wrong. I was trying to tell what had happened to me quickly and telling her that we should wake her mom. Tim was trying to tell her too. The stranger walked into the living room with his boots in his hand, his pants half pulled up and he was just pulling down his shirt from over his head. Alisha couldn't believe it! She yelled at him and said, "You got to get out!" It woke Ms. Towns. Ms. Towns was cursing at the stranger and pushing him out the door.

It was about four o'clock in the morning and Tim and I began to tell Ms. Towns and Alisha what happened. I couldn't stop crying and shaking. Alisha was hugging me and Ms. Towns began to cry and tell me how sorry she was. Ms. Towns called the police and my mother.

The police arrived right before my mother did. My mother brought one of the brothers from the mosque with her. The police and Bro. Kev were asking me questions. We gave a description to the police. It had only been 15 minutes since the stranger left and he was on foot so the police figured he couldn't have gone far. After the police left, Ms. Towns was still crying and she was apologizing to my mother, telling her how sorry she was. My mother and Bro. Kev told me I should've called them. They were talking to me like they were angry with me. Their tone was as if it was my fault. In my mind, it was like they were saying that I could've prevented it. I felt so helpless and like it was my entire fault. That is a huge burden for an 11 year old to bear. They made me feel worse than I had already felt but I never expressed it. They never found the stranger" (Murrell, 2015, p. 19 – 24).

This encounter was the beginning of my accelerated metamorphosis from youthful innocence to an unquenchable sex addict. I was not allowed to speak about the incident again nor receive any help or therapy to help me cope with it at the very least, let alone overcome it. The silence in itself was the accelerant. Anger, confusion, pain, depression, worry, and fear festered and grew stronger in my silence with every minute, hour, day, and week that passed. What if I ran into him on the street? What if he recognized me and wanted to finish what he started? What would I do? These were some of the questions I often asked myself.

I had no father to protect me, no mother to protect or avenge me, no one to speak up for me. It did not fully consume me yet, but little did I know, the sexual deviancy was going to set in, taking the place of my previous understanding of what love looked like, what value was, and whether or not I was worthy of either. After all, justice was something people on television went after and obtained. I never thought I had a chance.

Life at home just worsened. Another man had been added to the picture at home who happened to be a violent registered sex offender in more than one state. He was reckless with his threats and actions. My relationship with my mother and siblings began to deteriorate severely. This would continue for the course of a couple of years up until I left home at 15 ½ years old and well after that. We will get back to some of that a little later.

I became so depressed and just wanted to the pain to stop. I stayed up some nights laying in bed crying and pleading with God to let me die. I questioned why He would allow me to experience and feel all of what I had. Yes I had a roof over my head, yes my mother made sure we had food, clothes, and shoes, and yes I was a talented, pretty, honor student, but none of that mattered. Inside, I was hurting so bad and I couldn't make it stop. I tried running away from home. I tried telling what was happening. I tried pleading with my mother and nothing worked. I couldn't take it anymore so I decided I would take my own life silently. Nobody would miss me except for my grandmother maybe. She was my world, my other mother, but her ability to see what was really going on was clouded by the master performance put on by my mother.

I attempted to take my own life twice during this time. The first time, I decided I would overdose on some pills in my mother's top dresser drawer. I went into the bathroom with the pills because it was the most private room in the house. I began taking the pills one after the other and I had only gotten a few pills swallowed when one of my sisters knocked on the door and it startled me. I dropped the pills down the drain. When that didn't work, a week later, I decided I would try stabbing myself with a kitchen steak knife. I took it into the bathroom and began jabbing it into my stomach. It hurt but I just gritted my teeth. The knife would not pierce my skin! I cut my stomach up a little and had a few bruises but that was it. I became even more angry.

I began to become a little isolated in my thoughts and socialization as much as possible without raising any flags that may alert anyone that something was wrong after this next incident. I did not want to feel like it was my fault or even go through the feeling of disappointment again.

"There was a boy who lived in the same apartment community as my cousin Nancy whom I knew from school. He was a senior in high school. I was going to be a sophomore after the summer was over. His name was Monroe. He was 19 years old. I was going to be 16 in a couple of weeks.

Monroe wasn't a very cute guy but he was okay looking. He approached me and we began to talk on the phone. Even though he wasn't that cute, he seemed like a nice guy so we started to date. The only people that knew we were dating were Nancy and my Aunt Lisa. Monroe and I got along sometimes and then sometimes we argued.

Monroe used to talk about his mom and his little sister all the time but I hadn't met them yet. He talked highly about his mother and sister so I thought he had the utmost respect for females.

Monroe wanted me to meet his mother and his sister. One afternoon, Monroe asked if I would come over to his apartment to meet his mother and his sister. I was a little skeptical at first because I had never done anything like that before. We had only been talking for about 4 weeks. I went with him across the parking lot into the apartment. His mother and sister were home. He introduced us. His mother seemed like a very nice lady and his little sister was so cute and sweet. She was about 7. We all talked for a while, then his mother and sister had somewhere to go. I went to follow his mother and sister out the door and back to my cousin's apartment. He stopped me and asked me to stay for a minute while he got something. I was a little scared but I stayed. I sat in the chair in the living room.

Monroe came back into the living room and I stood up. I told him that my cousin was getting ready to leave in a little bit. We had somewhere to go. He asked me for a kiss. I said ok. I gave Monroe a kiss. Monroe started to wrap his arms around me and I began to get scared. I stopped and told him that I needed to get back across the parking lot. He gently grabbed my arm and asked me to stay for just a little bit. I told him no. I didn't want my aunt and my cousin to come looking for me. I started toward the door and Monroe pulled me by my arm a little rough. He wasn't violent but it was a firm pull on my arm. I thought about the stranger and what happened to me when I was 11 years old.

I don't think Monroe meant to try and force me but he wasn't understanding me when I kept telling him no. That made me afraid. He told me he wasn't going to let me leave until I came into his room. He said he wanted to show me his room. I wasn't stupid and I knew what that meant. It was just me all by myself in that apartment with him and I didn't have anyone else to run to or wake up this time. So I sat down on the bed and I was shaking a little. I tried not to show that I was scared. I figured I would go along with whatever he said and the sooner I did what he asked, the sooner I could leave. He touched my shoulder and felt that I was shaking and told me to relax. "I'm not going to hurt you", he said. "I promise I'll be gentle", he said. I told him that I was a virgin and I didn't want to do this. He told me to just relax in a firm tone.

I mean I was 15 and he was 19. He was much older than me and I was under age and I wasn't ready to do this. I had gotten myself into a situation that I didn't know how to get out of. I didn't know what would happen if I continued to refuse and I didn't want to find out. I didn't want to make him angry. So I pretended to be okay and I closed my eyes. I couldn't stop shaking though. He told me to lay back. He began to remove my pants and my underwear. I placed my hands over my eyes. He got on top of me and he began to have sex with me. I kept my hands over my eyes. I was quiet. I kept thinking about how bad it was hurting. It didn't feel good at all. With my hands still over my eyes, I said, "Please stop, it hurts." He told me to just relax and it only hurt because I was a virgin. He really thought he was doing something, but he was hurting me. I kept my hands over my eyes. He said, "What's my name?" I didn't say anything. He asked me again. I replied, "Monroe", with no feeling whatsoever. It seemed like this went on for a very long time but it only lasted about five minutes. When he was done a tear fell from my eye. He got up. I was silent. I got up, put my underwear and pants back on and left" (Murrell, 2015, p. 30 – 33).

This incident was the beginning of the sexual deviancy setting in. My character began to change and I became more moody and numb at the same time. I was so angry with everyone, but mostly myself. I couldn't even commit suicide successfully. Nobody took the time to ask me how I felt, if I was okay, or even if I needed any help. I couldn't take it anymore. I decided I would try one last time to commit suicide and would do so in a manner where I would surely succeed. "I took some Mean Green cleaner from the cabinet and poured it into a glass about half full. I mixed it with a little milk so that it would be easier to swallow. I was in the bathroom once again. I guess I liked going into the bathroom because it was the most private room in the house. I drank it down fast. I didn't feel anything at first. Trina, my best friend at the time had arrived and I left. I began to sweat and feel like my insides were on fire. Trina was driving to her mother's house. She looked over at me. I was moaning. She asked me what was wrong. I told her nothing was wrong and that I would be alright. I was hunched over in my seat. She raised her voice and demanded that I tell her what was wrong with me. I told her that I wanted to die and that I drank some house cleaner. Her eyes got so big. She couldn't believe it. She asked me why I would do such a thing. I told her she wouldn't understand. She told me that she was taking me to the hospital. I begged her not to. She said that she was going to tell her mother what I had done and she would know what to do. We pulled up in front of her mother's apartment. We entered the apartment and I immediately lay on the floor in a ball. My insides felt like they were going to fall right out between my legs. Trina's mom asked what was wrong. Trina told her what happened. Trina's mom told me that she was going to call my mother and tell her what I did and that she was going to take me to a hospital. It had been about an hour and a half since I drank the cleaner and I thought to myself, "What is taking so long?" I begged her not to call my mother and not to take me to the hospital. She gave me an ultimatum; either I let her call my mother and take me to a hospital or I could drink a lot of water to flush the cleaner out of my system and eat something. She wasn't going to have a teenager end up dead in her house on her watch. So I agreed to take the water and the food and she didn't call my mother. Trina asked me why I wanted to kill myself. I told her about the molestation and rape and the problems at home and I just couldn't take it. She was crying and hugging me and telling me that it was going to be alright and that she was there for me if I needed her. I appreciated her for that but I longed for that bond with my mother. I had already been abandoned by my father. In my mind, I asked God why He wouldn't just let me die" (Murrell, 2015, p. 37 – 38).

I remember thinking to myself the last suicide attempt was the reason I was diagnosed with a severe case of endometriosis. The doctors wanted to give me a hysterectomy at 15 years old. I was told there was a 75% chance I would not be able to have children. That added to my anger and frustration. I spent the rest of my teenage years and young adult life in pain because of this condition.

Shortly after the last suicide attempt, my mother put me out of the house after dropping me off at a child government facility because I would not conform to the chaotic and abusive atmosphere at home. I pretended to be alright in front of people, but internally, I was dying fast. The little girl inside of me was suffering. I quit singing at school, stopped playing sports, did not participate in after school activities or clubs. I was fading fast and yet, nobody noticed. I didn't enter into anymore talent shows either. I lost my courage, my voice, my mind, and my desire to live. By now I was just existing.

The sexual uncontrollable urges set in and I began to accept that I was not good enough to love, to be cared for or to be paid attention to so I began doing what I felt would simulate the feeling of love and gave into the uncontrollable thirst of needing to be wanted and touched. I went from being isolated to being addicted to sex and prescription drugs. I used my prescription as a way to escape emotional and physical pain since they were a narcotic.

Ed, Brian, and Paul were my first choice of drugs. Brian was the first drug. I completely lost myself. What is sexual deviancy? It is a condition where an individual is compulsively dependent on an unusual fantasy to be sexually aroused that is not acceptable socially and sometimes, personally. How did I get here? I would have remained a virgin until marriage and would not have had this difficult of a time finding out who I am and loving me in spite of had my innocence not been tampered with.

Brian and I did things like had sex in the park in daylight and at night on the tables, upside down in the swings, etc. I just stopped caring about respecting myself. Oh and the words coming from his mouth were so smooth. I was used to this kind of talk though so it did not even phase me though it sounded good and made me smile for the sake of "feeling" like I was truly wanted. Then when I was done with Brian, I needed another drug, so I chose Paul. He actually pretended to like me just to get me to have sex with him but once we began having sex for the first and only time, I demanded he get off of me in the middle of the act. I told him he didn't know what he was doing. I never saw or heard from him again.

I began to become careless with the feelings of others as well. Having sex felt good physically while it lasted and was like a cheap band-aid emotionally, because right after it was over, you realize the words spoken during sex were just for show and it did not ease the pain. It was like a small concussion mentally each time, because it confused me more about who I was and whether or not I was good enough for anyone to want and love.

I needed another drug so I began having sex with Ed. He liked me the moment he laid eyes on me. He was relentless in trying to get me to become his girlfriend but I wasn't in the mindset of settling down plus he and his girlfriend were on and off a lot and I definitely wasn't interested in sharing if I was going to settle down. We met a lot and had sex in the car in parking lots, at his house and more. I would tell him what he wanted to hear because he had this obsession with me and it was the only way to get him to stop trying to force me to be his. I liked him but he knew he wasn't going to have his cake and eat it too with me.

Here I am thinking I have gotten a grip on my ability to find a way to cope with everything by accepting this as all I deserve and am worth and then the worst happens. "I was wearing a black skirt with knee high slits up the sides, a grey and black casual button up shirt with my work shirt thrown over my shoulder and black casual rubber sole shoes. My hair was freshly styled and it was warm outside. My shift ended at 10:00pm and about 10 minutes had passed. The sky and the streets grew darker and the air began to fell muggy. I went back inside to call my cousin to see if she had forgotten to pick me up. No one answered. I got the feeling she forgot about me. I was 16 years old and though a teenager, I was scared to walk home in the dark when the walk would last an hour at minimum. I thought to myself I didn't have a choice. I needed to get home. So, I began to walk at a quick pace.

The streets were dark and I had a long journey ahead of me. After walking about 25 to 30 minutes, rain began to drizzle and I did not have an umbrella or jacket. I used my work shirt to cover my head. A few minutes later, as I was approaching the entrance of an apartment complex, getting ready to pass it, a stranger in a green Ford four door SUV approached. It was a man with three young female passengers. He asked if I needed a ride home. I remembered being taught to never talk to strangers or ride with strangers. I declined and tried to keep walking. He pulled up beside me and told me it was too last for me to be walking by myself and asked how old I was. I responded. He began telling me that the passengers were his daughters and they were on their way home, as he needed to get them in the bed, but would not mind giving me a ride home. One of the passengers looked to be about my the same age as me, and the others were a few years younger. Only two of the girls were awake. I felt a little scared, but it was very dark, raining, and it would take me forever to get home. I accepted and got into the truck. He began introducing me to the girls and asked my name and then told me I was a pretty young lady. I said thank you and he asked me where I lived. I told him where I lived and he said he knew exactly where it was and would get me home after he dropped his girls off at the apartment to get them in the bed. They lived in the apartments I had just been passing. I said okay.

He parked and they began to get out of the truck. I told him that I would wait outside in the truck. He said he would be a few minutes because he had to get his girls situated and asked me to come in. I was hesitant, but went in anyway. I don't know what was going through my head. I guess the fact he had daughters made me believe he wasn't going to try anything with me. As we walked in, he locked the door behind us and that frightened me. "Why would he be locking the door if we are going to head back out in a couple of minutes," is what I thought to myself. I sat down on the couch as he walked the girls to their rooms for bed. The apartment was very quiet and dark. He walked back into the living room and stood in front of me. I stood up and asked if we could leave. I told him my aunt would be very worried if I didn't show up soon. It was about 11:00 pm by then. He said before we left, he wanted to show me something. I became afraid. I knew something was not right and thought to myself it was going to happen to me again, only this time I was going to die afterwards. I contemplated dashing around him to the door, but I was scared he would catch me. I didn't know what would happen if I screamed, so I just begged him to please let me go home. He told me to calm down and grabbed my hand and started towards the back of the apartment. I began praying asking God, "don't let me die." I was being held against my will and tried to show no fear, but I was losing that battle quickly.

He was a slim man, average height, low fade, goatee, and chocolate brown skin tone. He smelled of a slight must and was trying to come across as a nice guy, but what he planned on doing to me was going to be anything but nice. He took me into a room where there was a black canopy bed. He closed the door and locked it behind us. I began to cry and told him I really needed to get home. He told me to relax and that I would be able to leave in a few minutes. He told me to lie down on the bed. I couldn't stop crying. I thought that if I just hurried up and did what he said, I would live and still be able to go home. I knew it was getting ready to happen to me again and I couldn't understand why me. He began to undress and I just lay there fully dressed with my eyes closed as tears ran down my face. He lay down next to me and began asking me questions about myself and where I was from while using his hands to unbutton my shirt and fondle me. I asked him to stop and to please let me go. He got on top of me and began undressing me and I cried and pleaded with him to stop. I was shaking uncontrollably and he told me to relax. He whispered, "I'm not going to hurt you." I heard that a lot as a child, but I always ended up hurt anyway. It seemed to be a universal term. I felt so low, dirty, and violated. I felt like I was nothing and a coward for not having the courage to fight back, because my fear of dying overpowered my fear of being raped. As he threw my clothes on the floor, still straddling me, he put his penis in my face and made me perform oral sex. I had no idea what I was doing and began to gag while crying and begging him to stop. He stopped and inserted his penis and began to rape me while he had one of his hands around my neck and telling me how beautiful I was. I lay there with a face full of tears blaming myself. It was my fault. Had I not gotten in the truck with a stranger, none of this would be happening to me" (Murrell, 2015, p. 52 – 56). When he was done with me, I remember him telling me to get dressed. I don't remember much after that. I have no idea how I made it home. I do remember not saying anything to anyone for years until a couple of year ago because I just knew I would be blamed for what he did to me. Yes, you heard me right. I was kidnapped, held against my will and raped. I should have died that night.

By now, I was completely removed from reality. I did find a cover up to hide the prescription drug addiction, anger, depression, fear, and everything else I was battling. I began doing hair and nails to keep myself occupied and my grades dropped slightly. I went from being a straight A student to an A and B student. The more I hurt, the more I used the pills to try and get the attention of my mother and anyone who would act like they cared about what was going on with me. I began taking them more and more, even when I was not in pain. I also began having more sex trying to fill a void that seemed like a bottomless pit. No matter how much I gave of myself physically, emotionally, and financially to young men, I could not find what I needed, whether they were a boyfriend or just a sex partner.

SEX HYPE:

Adults don't realize how much damage they cause when they silence children and teach them to hide what is or has happened behind closed doors. As a child, I felt so helpless and hopeless and completely alone. I felt like molestation and rape were normal after a while. I just figured it was something that happened to some people and you are just supposed to keep quiet, suck it up, and deal with it the best way you know how. I also began to associate sex with being wanted and loved. I thought the more I gave of myself, the more they would be open to caring about me, wanting me, and loving me.

I wanted so desperately to have the type of relationship with my mother that my cousin had with my aunt and to have the type of relationship with my father that my other cousin had with his dad. Because I could not obtain either one of these, I tried hard to obtain the equivalent of or higher level of love by trying to develop the type of connection or relationship with a man that my grandmother had with my grandfather. The only problem was, I didn't know how to obtain it. I also didn't realize I was looking for my father through sex as well.

I wasn't aware that sexual deviancy had fully set in until I began having sex with one young man one day and another young man the next day. I didn't realize how much I was starving for attention until I had one young man picking me up to take me out and as he was leaving, another one coming to pick me up to take me out too. They were barely missing each other. I cared nothing about whether or not a fight would break out or if feelings would be hurt. I only cared about fixing me.

It hadn't clicked completely that my sexual urges and addiction were not fixing the issue and was barely pacifying my desperate need.

3 SEXUAL HEALING

By now, Antwan had been added to the mix. He turned into a boyfriend. This is where I began to sex as a way to try and heal self by trying to turn sexual encounters, dates, and phone conversations into something meaningful, hoping to become healed from my pain. I wanted the depression, anger, and suicidal thoughts to go away. Rejection sent me back into a mental spiral every time. I wanted to be irresistible.

Antwan and I began having sex a lot and were in a relationship, Ed as well. He just couldn't let me go and he couldn't get enough of me. His relentless behavior made me feel like I was really worth something and though he kept telling me that he loved me and was in love with me, I think it was just fascination and lust. Antwan told me he loved me also. I heard this from a lot of guys. It was easier to believe it and "feel" loved than to not believe it and add to my emptiness.

I eventually stopped having sex with Ed and became fully involved with Antwan only. I was 16 ½ at the time. Antwan and I were having sex all the time at his house, in the car, at the movies, and so many other places. He began asking me about giving him oral sex and I did not want to. This is what the last rapist forced me to do but I needed to please Antwan if I wanted to keep him right? I made him promise to never leave me. I did anything he asked me to. I bathed him, had sex with him wherever and whenever he wanted. I was fearless in that regard.

Then there came a time when another young man who had a crush on me for a couple of years from the time he laid eyes on me reconnected with me. Antwan had begun selling drugs and smoking and cheating. I was not happy at all. I found myself paying for our dates, buying him gifts, and paying a car note or two while I didn't receive much of anything in return, but he, his penis, and his companionship was all I wanted and needed to be happy, to be loved. Each time I had sex with him, it was like an addict getting a fix. After all, I was an addict. Sex and pills allowed me to keep existing while trying to find my way through life. Because Antwan's behavior changed, I began entertaining CJ. He an I finally hooked up and we began having sex. He had a girlfriend too but told me he wanted me from the moment he saw me and wanted to be with me. I was a side chick on and off. He kept telling me he wanted to leave her for me. Once again, I was like an exotic piece of fruit. I fed into this. Another one wanted me, desired me, and needed me. This is what I needed to stay high and to be healed finally, right?

After a while of meeting up to have sex and listening to his sweet words, we lost touch after a while and Antwan and I broke up. I needed to find another drug to feel better and try to heal. I reconnected with yet another young man with whom I met in the 9th grade. I was 17 years old by now. Matt was what you call a church boy. He was such a gentleman. He wanted to be with me but he wasn't like the others. Sex was not his motive. He was sweet. He listened to me, we sang on the phone together, we hung out, and he didn't even try to kiss me. I wasn't used to this type of behavior and because I did not know how to respond or how to receive it, I felt like I wasn't getting what I needed. I felt like my addiction was not being fed and therefore, it didn't work out. I knew this was how a woman should be treated. I saw it with my grandmother and on television, but I thought that was for "good girls." I was damaged goods. I wasn't worthy of such treatment. I wanted to be worthy of it, but I couldn't change my past and had no idea how to change my mindset and get to a place where I didn't need sex to try to heal me.

Shortly after Matt and I stopped talking, I met JR. Boy was he persistent! He showed up at the different churches I would sing at and showed up at my house every single day and took me out a lot. Oh, did I forget to mention I was still going to church, but didn't know what it was to have a real relationship with God. I wasn't singing in the choir, but I did begin singing with a group of friends and did sing solos from time to time. I still had lost my voice in a sense to the point my passion for what gave me life (singing) seemed to fade away. I was trying to find it again.

JR was a church boy too. He was like a knight in shining armor. He said all of the right things and did all of the rights things too. He made me feel the most comfortable out of all of the young men I had been with. He was the first one, to know anything about my past. I told him everything. He said that I could trust him, he said he loved me, and he said he would always be there for me because he wasn't going anywhere. We began having sex as well, a whole lot. He made me feel good on the inside and physically too. We entered into a relationship. He introduced me to a new church family where I entered into a program for sexual abuse victims and it helped me. It didn't totally heal me, but it did help some. I was beginning to understand what it meant to have a relationship with God while attending this church and I loved it so much that I joined.

T   hings were going so well and I finally felt like my search for love was finally paying off. I gave JR all that I had. I poured my soul into the relationship which turned into marriage and two children. I decided to find out who I was as well. I wanted to give myself all that I had to learn what it was to be a woman, a mother, a wife, and healed. I spent many Sundays at the altar and attending different meetings at church that I felt could help me. It wasn't until 9 months into my marriage and 1 new born baby later that I realized there may have been some red flags I missed because I was so caught up in finding a savior to save me from the pain I was in. Infidelity became a normal behavior that I put up with in my marriage as well as lying along with verbal and emotional abuse. Now my husband was adding to the fire I was working so hard to put out.

Nine months into my marriage, my husband told me he didn't want to be married anymore and that he was moving out into another apartment. He moved another girl in with him and told me he was going to leave some clothes at home in case he wanted to come spend the night some times. I was so furious and extremely hurt at the same time. I had just given birth to our first child 6 weeks before. In my mind, I thought to myself, "who does he think he is and doesn't he know that plenty of men would kill to be with me?" I wanted to teach him a lesson. I reconnected with CJ and he began calling the house and my cell and we had sex one time. He told me how stupid JR was for treating me the way he did and for letting me go. JR became furious and jealous and exchanged words with CJ over the house phone. I felt like I was the reason he was behaving the way he did and so I blamed myself and tried harder to fix me. Though he decided he wanted his family after a few months and said things would change, he continued to cheat with countless women and I kept forgiving him. He even impregnated another young lady and yet, I felt I needed him so I stayed. I suffered through complete literal isolation, depression, STDs, infidelity, pornography, emotional abuse, verbal abuse, and towards the end of my marriage, physical abuse. Whether he was grabbing me by the arm or bending back my fingers when I threatened to leave with items from our house. Things got progressively worse but through it all, sex seemed to be the addiction both of us had. I had lost myself in him and began to somewhat worship him because my identity was tied to what he thought and felt about me. He had become my God in a sense. I had not acquired balance yet between my relationship with God and with him. I didn't even know who I was when I met him and was trying to find out while I was with him. I had enough and reached my breaking point when I was attempting to commit suicide with my 6 month old and 1 year old in the house. It was at this point, I decided I had to try and get my life together and heal a different way. I didn't want the cycle to continue with my children. I left JR.

I wanted to change, but I didn't know how to turn off the urges and the addiction. The things JR did once we separated and divorced sent my anger and depression to a 1000%! I was angry with God. I couldn't understand why He kept allowing traumatic things happen to me and why there was still something in me that was concerned more about others than myself. This was the point I accepted that I would never be valuable to any man, or to anyone. Experiencing unconditional love was never going to be a reality for me. Because I was so angry, I decided to leave church and do me. I turned my back on God and on my journey to finding self. I started wilding out! I was cold and heartless. It was time to get high again…..on sex. A sexual high is what I needed to feel better.

SEX HYPE:

The false belief that the more you give, the more you will get in return will cause you to make some extremely bad decisions. The belief that good sex and worshipping your man will make him remain faithful and have a desire to be kept by you is also a false belief. The belief that bearing his children will make him stay is also a false perception whether you birthed them out of love or intentionally out of desperation to make him stay.

When you are so damaged emotionally, mentally, physically, and spiritually, it clouds your ability to see what is wrong with self and definitely what you need to see in the other person. I later had to realize that I made the choice to enter into marriage without knowing who I was and saw man as my savior when he had not died or gave up his life for me. He didn't hold the key to my identity, purpose, assignment, or my healing and he surely could not love me because I didn't love myself first and neither of us understood what true love was to begin with.

I came to the realization that I too, played a role in the failure of the relationship as well as the addition to my pain because I chose to enter it and I allowed the behavior throughout it. I came to this realization years later. Sex was the thing both of us were addicted to especially when it came to each other, but it could not fix me or my marriage.

4 sexual high

Because I was so furious and hurt behind my divorce and the years of after math, I lost complete control behind the mask. Now, I just need to get high. Though JR and I were not on good terms, we continued to have sex on and off. Sometimes I would get caught up in my feelings because I still loved him and other times, it was just sex. I put myself in the mindset that I'll give you just enough of what you want, but you don't deserve the rest. I would dress sexy just to tempt him and would show up wherever he was or meet him and act like I was going to see another man and he would get pissed off. Other times, we would just have sex and go on about our way. He would try to talk me into marrying him again knowing he was having sex with other women. I still loved him and still wanted to have sex with him, but I wasn't going to enter into marriage with him again knowing he hadn't changed.

I started getting sexually high all of the time, even with men I wouldn't give the time of day to. This continued over the course of a few years. I continued to work on me little by little, but this was an area of true struggle for me. I started having sex with Marcus and Junebug first. Marcus was an old friend from high school and was talking about marrying me 4 weeks into talking to me. He moved me and my children into his house. I told him yes only to piss off JR. My children were in the middle of this mess. There were high speed chases, me being held against my will and so much other foolishness involved. Marcus ended up being a scam artist who went to federal prison. The game became a thrill to me and I just wanted him to hurt as much as he hurt me and I wanted to numb the pain.

Junebug was pure lust. We both were fresh out of a divorce and were at odds with our exes. I did stupid stuff like give him money, let him drive my car, etc. I was completely gone mentally and emotionally once again. We were having sex every other day. I needed it and he needed it and we were satisfying each other's craving.

Once I was done with Junebug, I moved on to Victor. Victor was not my type at all. If I wasn't so angry, I would have seen the deeper issues with Victor as well. He was a rebound person whom I actually married and got an annulment just to piss off JR. Yes. I was off the chain. He was physically abusive and I became pregnant with his child. He was arrested for battery on another woman and was so violent towards me before and during pregnancy, the judge granted a restraining order for me and my unborn child. This was the drug that got me in major trouble and caused me to go back to church and try to get back on track to work on me.

After Junebug, I met Albert. He was a smooth talker and a pretty cool guy. He flashed money and was telling me all that he could do for me, but little did he know, his money was not of importance to me. I did have my own money. Albert and I hit it off and we began having sex as well. I had no intentions on getting serious with Albert because I was trying to continue working on me. I knew that sex was a struggle for me. This turned into a relationship as well. I was a little better in regard to my relationship with God and a few issues I had with self, but I definitely wasn't where I needed to be.

I ended up getting pregnant with Albert's child. I had to make the decision to get an abortion a few weeks into my second trimester which was very hard and traumatic. I was depressed again. I murdered my own child. I ended up getting pregnant again with his second child and gave birth to my third child. I knew I should not have married him, but he became my second husband. Once again, I found myself in a marriage full of lies and infidelity. I found myself taking care of him as if he was one of the children as well and he became very abusive. Yet again, I was in another domestic violence relationship. I started to see a pattern. Not only did I experience this as a child at home, I had now lived it in several relationships. I noticed that I was no longer emotionally tied or invested in Albert or the marriage and I had to get out before one of us ended up killing each other and before my children were exposed for too long and ended up getting hurt in the process. We divorced. I was so tired of giving and loving and not getting the same in return. I knew that I desired a husband and a family, but I didn't want it like this. I knew there was much better but I just didn't know how to obtain it. I was so distraught about my current situation and I remembered reading in the word about the latter being greater than the past. This came to mind……..

LATTER

"Alone in the room. Loneliness fills the air and I am suddenly taken aback by my thoughts because I thought I had forgotten so easily what now seems to be branded into my mind, my vision.

Love that was proven to have seeped through the failed attempts of resolve began to show through the luminous memories that now fill my head.

And as I allow myself to become consumed with revisiting the bliss, a short circuit occurs and corrupt scenes begin to block my vision.

My heart becomes corroded with feelings of agony and it is not until the attack occurs; the undoing of every carefully sewn stitch begins to threaten my lifeline; living, loving, forgiving…..now all at stake.

Panicking as I try to get away from remembering why ties were severed at the core to begin with.

Then…… I see the latter enter and all chaos ceases only for me to realize I was never sitting here alone.

Tricked by he who comes to steal pure joy. Invading my thoughts persistently trying to persuade me the past is what I want.

Determinedly, I decline. The latter is what I need. Ooooh wee……he gone love him some me!" ~Jacquie Murrell

After Albert, I had to do some serious self-reflection and I was further than where I used to be as far as self and my relationship with God, but still wasn't where I used to be. I was financially stable, stable in my first business, and was doing so well healing and overcoming many things. The one area I struggled in the most, relationships and sex, was the area I needed the most work in. I continued to settle and kept thinking my actions would help change a man and it just wasn't true. God showed me a lot about self that I just wasn't ready to see but that I needed to see. It was the beginning of me truly learning to love all of me, make it a habit to self-reflect and make the necessary steps to change for the better, and swallow my pride. I didn't want help from anyone but losing everything and being at my lowest with all four children is what God used to get me by myself to get my attention.

As I began my journey, I had to prostitute self for a place for me and my children to lay our heads. I had to be strong, do what I needed to do to survive and cope through the transition while working on self. I began having sex again with JR and once again, that ended in disaster.

Sex had now become more of a coping or stress reliever mechanism like a cigarette rather than a means to heal. The healing process from my childhood had already taken place, but now I needed healing from the relationships I had been in. Forgiveness had become a regular thing to which I had now become accustomed to. This made my ability to keep moving forward easier.

I had completely stopped having sex with JR. I found myself choosing a different drug to help me with stress and my drug of choice this time was Sly. Sly was a sweetheart and someone I had recently connected with from high school. He needed a little bit of help with money and a ride to and from work and so I helped him out as much as I could. He expressed that he has always had a crush on me but felt I wouldn't give him the time of day. We started hanging out and having sex too. We had sex at my office and a lot of it. I felt myself getting emotionally attached and I decided to end it because he deserved better than me. My next drug of choice after Sly was Gus. Gus and I were friends in high school and he moved away. When he returned, we reconnected and we decided that we both were dealing with some things and needed to just satisfy the sexual urges and agreed we would just be sex buddies exclusively. We talked a lot about life and had sex two to three times a week at his house. This lasted for a few months and then I decided I was going to try to be celibate. I was trying to overcome this struggle in my life. Everything else had gotten so much better and God knew this was an area that had been a major struggle since the moment I began to be sexually violated. From the fondling of my breasts, vagina and butt to the hands all over my body and the hard, unwelcomed thrusts of unfamiliar penises into my virgin vagina breaking my hymen, to watching the blood pour into my panties and down my leg, to being kidnapped, to the painful anus sex during rape, to the forced action of me having to masturbate in front of one of my rapists, to the forced

30

oral sex I was made to perform and the oral sex performed on me, all at the ages of 11, 15 and 16......it all played a role in making my sexual experience dirty, deviant, and premature. I didn't get to follow through with my choice of keeping my virginity until marriage and to have a pleasant and healthy sexual experience. It was like a demon had entered my body and consumed me with a sexual fire and desire I did not ask for while telling me over and over this is the closest you will ever get to love. I needed sex like we need oxygen to breathe. I began thinking to myself, "this is going to be the one thing that I struggle with for the rest of my life."

Celibacy lasted for about a couple of months and then I started losing the fight to control my urges. Even in celibacy, I also started doing things I never did before the last time I was raped. The sexual urges were too strong and I thought as long as I fight the need to have sex with a man, I am one step closer to beating this. I began fondling myself with my own hands to minimize the thirst. I masturbated sometimes twice per day 3 to 4 times per week. I did the some of the same things to myself that others did to me in the bedroom. I used ice, syrup, candlewax and more to try to quench the thirst, but it was not the equivalent of having sex. I loved the feeling of a real penis inside of me. It seemed to be the only way I could be totally satisfied every time I needed a fix.

I reconnected with someone from middle school this time and his name was Anthony. Anthony was in a relationship but was having problems and reached out to me on social media. He wanted to marry the woman he was with, but he needed help on how to deal with the issues. I will say that God gave me a gift to be transparent and to use my life experiences to help people. I was a walking manifestation of His love, grace, and mercy.

We met up and caught up on life and he told me about his problems and I gave him advice. He also expressed to me that he had always had a crush on me and would like to explore his fantasies of being with me. I obliged. He came to my house in the mornings before dawn to have sex with me. Sometimes, we even met up at a mall parking lot to have sex in the car. This lasted for a few weeks and then I cut it off. Over the years, I was very careful not to bring any of these men around my children. They were either not present or sleeping.

I tried to go back to being celibate but again, it only lasted a few months. This time, I masturbated much less than I did before. I felt like I was making progress. I began talking to a man named Jimmy. I knew him as a friend of a family of one of the guys I had been with. He was a delight to talk to. He had the best conversation and that was probably because he was several years older than me. We talked for days and we decided that we would become sex buddies. These men agreed to just fulfill a need and meanwhile, I was still putting my life back together slowly, but surely. We had sex about 3 times per week at wee hours in the morning right after he got off work. He showed me some things in the bedroom I had not yet experienced too and that just added to my thirst. I knew a whole lot already and was not afraid to try anything at least once in the bedroom. We had sex for months and then I decided I wanted to try and get back on track with my celibacy. During the time of being celibate this time, I had a birthday come up and I decided to go to a meet and greet for a social media group to get out. I didn't go out much. I basically went to work, school, church, and spent time with my children. Upon meeting someone I had talked to several times before on social media and once on the phone, we decided we would go back to his place. His name was Ron. I was comfortable since he wasn't a total stranger. Though I had never met him in person, I had interacted with him on several occasions which didn't cause me to feel threatened or like he would hurt me. Going home with strangers was not and would never be something I would be able to do. One night stands just were not my cup of tea.

I told Ron I had never done anything like that before, go home with someone I had just met in person though we had met on social media. He said I should live a little and made me feel comfortable. We had sex that night and continued to have sex and developed a really good friendship. He was going through a divorce at the time as well. We both went our separate ways after a while and lost touch.

I decided to try the celibacy thing again. It seems as though it was a game to me, but if you could switch lives with me, you would understand the struggle. Praying, fasting, pleading for it to get better, was not working. There were times I kept myself longer than others and I had reached a point where I was not even masturbating period. I felt like I was ready for a real relationship this time now that I was aware of who I was and was. Truth be told, I wasn't confident in it just yet. I still used my money and giving spirit to try and fix men and change them into what I needed them to be hoping they would want me and truly love me. Sometimes, I even continued to overextend myself to prove that I was good enough hoping they would see my worth and would want to keep me. My mother's and her husband's words rang clear as day in my ear throughout this whole process, "you are a porn star, you are only good to lay on your back, nobody is going to want to keep you or love you." Looking at my life, those words seemed to be true.

SEX HYPE:

Sometimes the hurt we endure can be so intense that we become so angry to the point we lose our ability to think rationally. Sex went from being a way to find love and feel loved to a stress reliever and coping mechanism. How does one rid themselves of so many devious sexual spirits and pain from trauma after trauma after trauma after trauma? It takes time, prayer, dedication and determination to change, and a strong will to want to be better so you can experience better as well as give better. It takes a whole lot of forgiveness and getting back up each time you fall, even if you fall a million times.

The sexual addiction was much stronger than the drug addiction. The withdrawals caused a strong sexual tingling sensation all over my body and anxiety. If I ignored the tingling and tried to keep myself occupied, it seemed like there were times it calmed down a little but rose up even stronger until I satisfied it and other times it just wouldn't stop unless I satisfied it. It was like nicotine. While other areas of my life flourished, I talked to God a lot about this struggle and asked God, "why is my struggle so different from others and why is it so hard?" I wanted to know why me. The more I had sex, the more I needed it and the less I had sex, the more I needed it. It didn't matter that I was no longer using it as a tool to find love anymore, but as a coping mechanism and a stress reliever. It wasn't fixing the issues and it wasn't helping the addiction.

5 situationships

It is now the end of 2012 and I have reached a point where I have been celibate for a few months and I feel like I know who I am, I know my purpose and I am ready to start dating. I still had a bit of a trust issue but I was still working on that. I was and had been stable since losing everything in the beginning of 2012 after my divorce from Albert.

I met a man named Deon on a social media platform one day. I should have known by his nickname on his profile that all he would want was sex, but I tried to give him the benefit of the doubt since he was the most respectful out of the guys that viewed and responded to my profile. We exchanged numbers and talked for a few weeks over the phone and decided to meet. He lived about 40 mins away from Indianapolis and I drove every other weekend and sometimes every weekend to see him. We hit it off. We began having sex and I noticed he was more of a sex addict than I was. He wanted two and three times a day every day. He prided himself on the size of his penis because it definitely was well outside of the normal and/or average size. The sex was great but, as time went on, he would lie about having other women over and yet I continued to "help" him financially and listen to him introduce me to others as his fiancé. He said he wanted to marry me but I told him I wasn't ready for that. This lasted for a few months but I got tired quickly. I had already been down this road and I wasn't trying to go there again. I was learning! This was a situationship.

I decided that I would go back to being by myself and then I met George on social media as well. He was a nice guy, handsome, and rough around the edges. He thought he was going to play with me like he did so many other women, but he wasn't banking on me being the woman that would help him turn his life around, support his dreams, and help him obtain the things needed in order to be successful. This was a situationship turned relationship. Now George was a different kind of guy because he too was abused during his childhood and grew up with some of the same issues and even worse environment than mine, so we understood each other. Because of his background, he too had a sex addiction. We tried to fight it but that didn't last long at all. I noticed I still had a little bit of lack of control in this area and I was fighting tooth and nail to master it. Sex was our favorite thing to do and then he proposed to me 3 months later in front of a packed pub and eatery and I said yes. I felt like my life was finally back on the right track and that I had found true love finally, but then something happened.

I found out that George had begun going back to some of the same lifestyles he used to have. Though he still went to church and took care of home, he lied to me and cheated on me. I was so hurt and would not take him back. I loved him, but I had to accept that was not who God had for me and no matter how much I invested in him, if he could not love me enough to respect our relationship and appreciate the woman who has been there for him for everything, then I could not stay. Before, I would have stayed through anything like I had done previously, but I was in a place now that I understood God was my God and that I was worth more and I was not afraid to be by myself. I didn't need sex or a man to be happy, sex was merely a stress reliever and coping mechanism when I was not in a relationship. I understood that I had to love me more. I was getting better at this.

After about 6 months, I met a man named Moe on social media as well who lived over 600 miles away. He was a handsome man of God and we exchanged numbers and began to talk. He was fresh out of a divorce too. It seemed that every man I met was in a place in his life of some type of transition that required an investment of some type from me and I kept falling for the ones who were supposed to be assignments. I went to visit Moe a lot and help with some very serious life issues he was dealing with. I visited on a bi-weekly and weekly basis by car and plane. I became attached to his children and we began doing relationship like activities as a couple and having sex but claimed not to be in a relationship. I found myself investing so much time, money, soul, love, and sex that I began to expect more from him. I cared deeply for him and he broke my heart in this situationship. I left him alone and months later he asked for another chance and said he didn't realize what he had until it was gone. Moe was a very materialistic man and struggled with identity issues and things made him feel like he was somebody. He too had an issue with sex. I gave him a second chance and it only took one time for him to blow it before I dismissed him and cut him off completely! It hurt because I loved the children, but I was starting to see that I believed who I was and knew my worth and would not settle. I also noticed that my sexual urges lessened.

A year later, I met a man named Larry. Larry was sure enough a fast talker. He could sale you your own underwear if he had to. Larry was an opportunist, liar, thief, and moocher. I couldn't see this at first because he is very good at disguising himself as a wolf in sheep's clothing. I tried to help Larry so much that I noticed my sincere desire to help him was what he used to talk his way into leading me on just enough to get me to like him but not enough to where he was willing to do what he needed to do to be in a relationship. I did have sex with Larry a few times, but he couldn't do anything for me so a relationship was out of the question. Once I caught on to what he was trying to do, I ended that situationship quickly and let's just say it ended with a restraining order.

I went back to my little life corner and continued to be great. I continued running my businesses, taking care of my children, steadily building on my relationship with God, enjoying being healed from past hurt and my marriage and was just enjoying life. I even went back to being completely celibate. I didn't even masturbate nor did I have the desire to. I had finally conquered the basic ability to function in a healthy manner. I was so tired that I told God not to allow me to cross paths with nobody else. I just wanted to stay single and rest in his arms though I know I had the makings of a wife. I had experienced enough life, fought enough battles and obtained wisdom and the ability to be transparent to help others. I knew what it was to support, invest, sacrifice, multiply, forgive, compromise, pray, maintain, etc. all while keeping Him first and all while continuing to allow Him to work on me. I told God, don't you send me nobody either. I'm done! Please Lord just let me be great with you!

Jacquie Murrell

SEX HYPE:

When you come into the understanding of who you are and what your purpose is and you are confident in that and can own it, you are not so easily inclined to accept anything less. After you have encountered as much hell as I have, you no longer have patience for things that will cause you to go backwards and you learn how to make better decisions. You learn how to take responsibility for your role in situations and figure out how you can do better next time. This is where I was.

Sometimes we fall for the assignment. I was the teaching woman. I helped so many in different areas and all they did was take because that was all they were meant to do in that season when crossing paths with me. I couldn't see that until after the situation was over. I was trying to make it into something it was never meant to be.

When you have truly been healed, you don't feel like you need to make one man pay for what another has done. You don't feel like you need to give up self to prove how worthy you are to be loved and be his wife. You don't feel like sex is needed to make the relationship work or hold it together. You understand that if his treatment of you and his actions don't mimic God's love for you, then you have no issue with walking away. You understand that it was not a loss, but a gain.

6 love finally

It is now the spring of 2015. I have just released my first book of a
three-part series entitled Life Support. This book is not just my life
story, but it is also a tool for those trying to overcome the same
obstacles and hardships that I defeated. Things like homelessness,
abandonment issues, anger, depression, suicidal thoughts, abortion,
divorce, rape, molestation, sex addiction, drug addiction, and more are
all in this series and are a part of the fight of life for so many. I was so
proud of me and though I was ridiculed and hated for releasing my
truth by some, I was celebrated and thanked by so many who have or
had been dealing with any of these issues. I had to learn how to
distance myself from people who were toxic to my environment and
life. I had gotten great at cutting people off, forgiving them and loving
them from a distance.

People wanted and needed to know how they too could overcome. I
was happy to finally be in a place where I was able to be 100%
transparent without caring what others thought or said about me, what
I chose to share and what I had been through. This gave me next level
freedom and healing. I felt completely liberated.

The Summer of 2015 was amazing. I had been doing excellent in
keeping myself. It had been about 2 years up until this point where I
finally was confident in and knew who I was, what I was purposed to
do, and life was great! I had my ups and downs like anyone else, but I
was stronger, wiser, and better all because of my determination to
never give up. I knew my worth. I made self-reflection and self-
maintenance a part of my routine and I was constantly using my story
to help others by speaking to groups and conducting Life Support
sessions at different facilities in addition to working with families one
on one.

I began interviewing on radio, television and podcast shows. Through
these opportunities, I became friends on Facebook with Mark Brooks.

Now he was not one of those men who was trying to get my number or get in my pants. We had the occasional conversation on Facebook within a group while discussing a topic and even met in person after running into each other in public while attending different events. I had absolutely no romantic interest in him, nor did I think he had any in me. From the summer of 2015 to Fall of 2016, Mark and I had several conversations occasionally. He inboxed me prayers from time to time and sent messages just to check up on me and then it happened……..he let it be known on social media that he was interested in me while participating in a group game. You know, the one where it asks "who would you date in this group." Of course, he tagged my name out of all of the other women in the group. Now at first I laughed and thought it was cute and went on about my business, but he made it a point to inbox me and let it be known that he was not joking and was interested in getting to know me. Now, I had been turning down guys left and right because I just was not interested in dating, relationships or giving my heart ever again. It wasn't because I was still hurt or bitter, but because I was just tired and wanted nothing to do with going through the motions of starting over in that area. I wanted to keep focusing on my children and business. Love from a man was no longer a goal of mine in that season. I desired a husband but didn't want to go through the necessary steps, ups and downs to obtain that. I was truly burnt out from all of the mess I had experienced.

Something told me to just respond and give him a shot. I did and it started a whirlwind. We began talking for hours on the phone and on our first date, we talked for hours until the restaurant closed. The next few times we talked on the phone and went on dates, it seemed like the conversations were endless, seamlessly going from one subject right into another. He exposed me to treatment I had not been accustomed to but that I had always desired. I was so uncomfortable at first because opening doors ALL OF THE TIME, compliments, not allowing me to lift certain things or repair certain things, checking to see if I have eaten, and so much more was just way outside of what I used to. Sitting and talking and having his undivided attention and receiving random texts throughout the day were among a few things that made him more and more interesting and desirable to me. His conversation and intellect made him the sexiest man I had ever encountered. The support, kind treatment, spiritual covering, and affection drew my heart to his hands.

I know you're probably thinking, "wasn't this the same chick that was so emotionally and mentally disconnected completely?" Yes. It's the same chick! I was feeling him and he was feeling me and had no problem with expressing that. We decided to enter into a relationship and this man treated me like a queen. I thought to myself, "girl, Jacquie what are you doing?" It didn't take long for me to develop feelings for him and then grow in love with him. I don't like the phrase, "fall in love."

I knew that keeping myself sexually was always going to be a challenge for me. You know we all have that one thing or two things that we will struggle with throughout our life that makes us imperfect and this was mine. I couldn't change what happened to me and how it affected me, but could continue to get better in my approach to overcoming it. I shared this truth with him and told him that I was trying to keep myself and wanted to proceed if he was okay with that, because I knew it was definitely going to be a major challenge now that I was attracted to him on every level. He understood and I began to think this is just too good to be true.

As time went on, I began to learn that he too had his share of challenges and hurt in relationships and marriage and because I am a giver and servant by nature and loved him, I wanted him to be able to experience everything he hadn't but deserved. I made it by business to treat him with the care, love, attention and respect he deserved.

Bringing our children into the equation was amazing. They all got along together so well as if they had already known one another and I was happy. I was truly happy for the first time in my life in the realm of love and romantic relationships. Could this truly be Love Finally?

To this day, we are still together. It has been over 2 years since we first met but a little over a year since we began our love journey together. We have our challenges and disagreements like any other relationship but we face them together and that is what makes us stronger. I know it isn't easy dealing with me and yet he exercises patience consistently.

This is what I have been looking and longing for almost my whole life and I found it in Mark Brooks Sr.

If I could sum up the way he makes me feel, how he makes me better, and what he adds to my life, it would sound something like this:

ONLY YOU

I imagined the day I would get to take my hand and gently stroke the side of your face
With His deeply embedded grace that lies in every inch of my being.
Tapping into the love and space reserved only for you
Making sure that it penetrates your heart with every word that leaves my lips,
Every gaze that leaves my eyes and every touch felt with my hands.
The mere presence of you here in this place under where the Almighty resides
Allows me to be comfortable with revealing myself in its purest form.
HE loves me so selflessly that HE decided to go a step further
And reincarnate HIS physical being in you….. the epitome of his love for me.
He thought I was worth keeping so HE whispered the secrets of my heart into yours
And here you stand before my eyes, taking residence in my being and being rooted in my soul.
Fighting with every fiber of my being not to lose control
Never realizing you being the tool used to help fuse the pieces of me thought to be left without a trace
While HE secretly prepared in my heart, your space and because of the time and tears that it took,
I can't help but think that maybe…..just maybe someone else should be written in this chapter in this book
Could this really be? He made sure that the transition would equip me with the faith to look
Even after all the hell HE allowed me to encounter, He still saw fit to make the decision that my season of consistent repetition of heartache and pain must come to an end
So this new season of the reciprocation of real love can begin
And even though many years of lies, misuse, abuse and mishandling of me were embedded in my veins
His love came in….a vaccination to counteract the poison that sought to flood the walls of my heart and soul
And it wasn't until then I realized that I never had control

Because what looked like death of a pure heart was really transformational sleep
While He breathed a brand new love and life into me and that's what He needed others to see
Because it wasn't until then, I was totally free
As if none of the infections that flooded my heart existed and it was as if I never even saw myself as damaged goods
Because He mended from within so it wouldn't show on the outside in a way that only He could
Then, I didn't know why this suffering existed for a transformation such as this, but now I do
Most of what we go through is not for us alone and His reason for this.....well, it was all for you
If I only knew that all of that was preparing me to wholeheartedly love you
It was hard to keep loving with all of those pieces, He knew that just wouldn't do, not for you or me too
So he tailored my thoughts, spirit, word, action & strength so they'd fit
......ONLY YOU
~Jacquie Murrell (Lady J)
My LOVE FINALLY.........Mark B.

SEX HYPE:

While this was a short account of just some of the things I experienced and participated in, it paints a clear picture of sexual healing failure. If I took the time to write every intricate detail and experience in regards to this method of "healing" a lot of people use, I would be writing another bible. As you can see, overcoming or being healed from sexual trauma, abandonment, and all of the aftermath that comes with it, cannot be accomplished by jumping from bed to bed. Though this behavior was developed by different traumas and experiences that planted a seed of sexual deviancy, had there been some help, tools, and guidance given; a lot of it could have been avoided. I became emotionally handicapped, mentally broken and spiritually dead. I even tried to take myself out physically several times and it seemed as if my condition and circumstances just kept getting worse. Every time I had sex with someone, it sent me on a high and then as soon as it was over, I came back down. I still saw myself as ugly, dirty, unlovable, unworthy, and damaged goods. I found myself being rude and telling young men to get up in the middle of sex because they didn't know what they were doing. I found myself having sex in the daylight out in the open on tables, chairs, swings, cars malls, etc. and all over the place as well as during the evening and I had no self-control. It truly was stronger than the prescription drug I was addicted to and it took over because my need to feed my void was interfering with my ability to make sound decisions.

I cannot stress enough to everyone, but especially young women, that using your body to obtain love, keep a man or woman, or heal hurt will only add to the challenge of finding yourself, loving yourself, and healing from the pain of the past. All of the different spirits, energy, personalities, and experiences collide and clash causing chaos and creates the inability to control your reactions to other painful experiences. Flipping out after choosing to stay with someone you know doesn't want you or respect you by fighting, screaming, cutting tires, lying about being hit, and all of the other drastic desperate reactions is due to what you allow into your being. Your mind, body and spirit are all connected. You cannot pray for a husband or be in a committed relationship with a "good man" and you have not gotten self together first. You will hurt him and ruin him. It is not enough just to be in a position to give love, you have to be in a position to receive it and truly know and understand what love is.

Programs for victims of sexual abuse, confidants, accountability partners, women's etiquette programs and other resources were what I used to help get me through this seemingly impossible war within myself. I may have lost many battles, but I won the war.

I can't truly express the awe and love I feel being with the man I have today. I never thought it would be possible for me, but God saw fit otherwise and I am forever grateful. Though we are both imperfect, he is perfect for me. Do I still struggle with little things? Of course I do, but I never stop trying. Now I coach and mentor others that have experienced traumas and are struggling with sexual addiction and other issues as this is only a small part of my story. Helping others gain total freedom to love self, love others and receive love is the ultimate goal. Never forget that healing requires your relentless participation. Nobody can obtain it for you. You have to want it and be willing to do everything you need to do in order to get it.

If you want to learn more about my story and the other life experiences I've had and how I overcame them all, you'll have to read the Life Support series (Part 1- Surviving Life's Worse Challenges and Part 2- Rehab). Part three coming soon!

ABOUT THE AUTHOR

Jacquie Murrell is an author, entrepreneur, speaker, mentor, life coach, radio and television personality, and mother. She holds degrees in Business Management and Psychology as well as certifications in tailoring and patient services. She is currently in the Masters/Doctorate program at University of Phoenix for Psychology.

Life's challenges compelled her to merge her experiences with her education to help others and so the Life Support book series was born. After overcoming abandonment, molestation, rape, homelessness, addiction, suicide attempts and much more, she fought to live. The series led to the opening of Life Support Company LLC in which she mentors and coaches young people and families, participates in events as a speaker, and helps people build and grow their businesses.

She now uses Life Support to encourage others to fight to overcome every obstacle and make their dreams a reality as she has. Being the founder/president of a nonprofit in Indianapolis, IN, business owner of a credit consulting group, CEO of a radio station, owner of a television and film production company, and a radio and television personality exhibits just a few accomplishments that only touch the surface of who she is and how powerful her story is as a direct result of her tenaciousness.